Construction Site Mission: Demolition!

SHERRI DUSKEY RINKER AND AG FORD

chronicle books · san francisco

Where a building's old and crumbling,
five big trucks all roll up, rumbling—
the sign says "Danger! Stop! Keep Out!"
But Bulldozer gives a thunderous shout.

Gates open wide, the trucks roll in,
they're revved and ready to begin!

Mighty Flatbed joins the crew—
she brings Skid Steer and Loader, too!

That rickety building has to GO!
They'll wreck it, rip it, blow-by-blow.
They can't wait to get underway:
This is DEMOLITION DAY!

Crane Truck, standing firm and tall,
swings a giant wrecking ball.

His aim is steady, sure, and straight—
he hits his target with the weight.

Concrete sails everywhere,
clouds of dust shoot through the air!
Crane sets up for another hit,
and beams and pipes and chimneys split!

He bashes through a concrete wall . . .

Now with his hook, Crane Truck will start sorting rubble, part by part.

With nice, neat piles, there's no doubt
that nothing good will get thrown out!
Metal, concrete, steel, and wood—
they'll be recycled, like they should.

Now Excavator takes the lead:
His bucket rams a wall, full speed. *SMASH!*
With each crash, each mighty thrust,
concrete and glass explode to dust!

He switches gears and turns around,
and sets his bucket on the ground.

Now a grapple helps him grip,
to tear and pull, to bite and rip.

Rebar, torn out without trouble,
concrete and steel, turned to rubble.

Now everything gets sifted through
to be reused for something new.

Dump Truck and Flatbed, working hard,
are hauling huge loads from the yard. *Honk! Honk! Roar!*
Everybody does their share,
to clear the site, to make it bare.

Crushing as he rolls along, *MASH!*,
Front End Loader's big and strong.
Rubble mashed beneath his weight
compacts as he rolls strong and straight

He lifts up giant chunks he's found,
and smashes them onto the ground.
Back and forth, he never quits,
'til everything is bashed to bits!

He hauls away the cracked debris,
and separates it carefully,
sorting metal, brick, and pipe—*and then*,
it's all saved, to be used again!

Little Skid Steer runs and races

through the site and in tight places.

Her breaker bit can shatter rock!

Her grapple pulls down cinder block!

Her bucket helps her dig and haul.

Her big blade can push through it all!
Vroom!

She revs up, she rolls, she *bashes*!
She busts a wall, and *THUD!* it crashes!

The crew batters, shatters, shakes—destroys!
The air is filled with smoke and noise.

CRUMBLE! CRASH!—And just like that,
the big old building is now FLAT! *Chhhhh!*
A dust cloud rises, falls, then clears,
the building's DOWN. The whole team cheers!

Now the crew works as a team,
to get the site all clear and clean.

They haul materials away,
to be reused, another day.

Then Big Bulldozer rolls around—
he levels land and clears the ground.

Vroom!

Cement Mixer pours some new concrete. *Chhhhh!*
The site is clean, all fresh and neat.

They've all worked hard to clear the space
so something *new* can take its place . . .

The day is finished—job well done!
Demo day was tough—but fun!
The tired trucks have done their best,
and now it's time to get some rest.

Tomorrow, there's more work to do—
they'll start building something new!

Now they'll dream of engines, rumbling,
wheels turning, rubble tumbling.

They'll dream about tomorrow, too—
the dirt and noise, the jobs they'll do,
of friends and work and all that's right . . .

Another good day.

Now, *goodnight.*

For Nancy Rinker—Mom, your support, enthusiasm, and
excitement have made this journey even more of a blessing.
Thank you for all you do. (Oh, and, "Hi, Dr. Packo!") —S. D. R.

For my nephew, Jireh, the newest baby boy in our family —A. F.

Text copyright © 2020 by Sherri Duskey Rinker.
Illustrations copyright © 2020 by AG Ford.

Library of Congress Cataloging-in-Publication Data available.

ISBN 978-1-4521-8257-5

Manufactured in China.

MIX
Paper from
responsible sources
FSC™ C104723
FSC
www.fsc.org

Design by Jennifer Tolo Pierce.
Typeset in Mr. Eaves San OT.
The illustrations in this book were rendered
in Neocolor wax oil crayons.

10 9 8 7 6 5

Chronicle Books LLC
680 Second Street
San Francisco, California 94107

Chronicle Books—we see things differently. Become part
of our community at www.chroniclekids.com.